SARA'S SECRET

Just like Sara, everyone has something to Hide for one reason or another. It could be a secret they are ashamed of and believe they have to hide it due to fear of what others may think of them. Many would prefer to take their secret to their grave at any cost, but sometimes their secret would escape, and they are shocked to find out that it was 'no big deal' or could inevitably be for their good.

"WHO WILL SAVE THIS QUEEN"
(*INTRIGING*)

HOWELL ALLEN

A

DEDICATION/HONOR

I must give honor to the Almighty Creator, my ancestors, for the extreme and enormous sacrifices they made for me to be here today, expressing my creativity. I am truly grateful for my creative and comedic talents, and my wisdom, knowledge and understanding, and the privilege to share my talents and creativity with the world.

CONTENTS

CHAPTER	TITLE	PAGE #
1	Meet Sara Levy	Pg #9
2	Sara's Childhood	Pg #10
3	Sara's First Engagement	Pg #11
4	Sara Got A Job	Pg #12
5	Sara 9th Engagement?	Pg #13
6	Sara Is Pregnant	Pg #14
7	Sara's Baby	Pg #15
8	Fun Girl Sara	Pg #16
9	Sara's Looks	Pg #17
10	Sara's Morals	Pg #18
11	Sara – The Daughter in law	Pg #19
12	Is Sara a Nymphomaniac	Pg #20
13	Sara the Story Teller	Pg #21
14	Sara's Curry Chicken	Pg #22
15	Sara's Taxi	Pg #23
16	Sara On The Radio	Pg #24
17	Sara The Movie Star	Pg #25
18	Sara The Pig Farmer	Pg #26
19	Sara On TV	Pg #27
20	Sara And The Married Men	Pg #28
21	Sara Turns To Jesus	Pg #29

E

ACKNOWLEDGEMENT

I would like to acknowledge and thank my three children, Nickesha Allen, Howell Allen Jr, and Kenola Allen for always giving me the drive and motivation to write and create new things. Once again, let me say thank you and one love!. Wishing you long life, peace, love, wealth, joy and happiness.

INTRODUCTION

Saving Sara is a book about a very, very beautiful lady named Sara, who has some secrets she would prefer to die with than to reveal to anyone.

After years of roller-coaster rides with many, many, many men, she met one man, name Joshua, who deciphers her problems on his own and assures Sara he will endlessly love her regardless.

Just like a true prophet, Joshua told Sara the truth about herself and had Sara kicking and screaming for months. Sara believed Joshua didn't know her well enough, and could not possibly discern her; he had only met her a short while ago. Sara was enraged... Sara stabbed Joshua, Sara put him in jail, Sara loathed him, Sara cursed him like a dog, Sara dashed dirty water in his face, Sara stopped talking to him.... Sara was mad as hell with Joshua, but, she still yearned to hear every word Joshua had to utter. Joshua was also a very, very, funny man. He didn't just come around regularly with his mind full of truth. He had Sara laughing most of the time, but when the facts are necessary, he delivers; And, Sara often rejects the package and tries to kill him. Joshua didn't stop until Sara accepted the truth that she knew would set her free, and give her the stability to lock up her open vagina shop and avoid being used.

H

Chapter 1

Meet Sara Levy

Sarah Levy. Sara Levy was born on December 4, 1987, in Clarendon, Jamaica. She was my next-door neighbor in Jamaica, and by coincidence, we end up living in the same building in Brooklyn.

Sara is a girl with the look, poise, and attitude of a Playgirl, but is still the girl next door. A total package! Sara always acts and appears to be in the driver's seat, but no one can ever figure out where she is going. In the area where she grew up, folks admire her friendliness and nice stride. Very cute - "pig wobble"-like steps turn everyone's head. She exemplifies the naturally carved out body and face of a supermodel. I always called her: "God's Top Model".. She looks absolutely perfect, just like a trophy!...

So, what is it that this perfect looking woman has to hide? What is Sara's secret?

Chapter 2

Sara's Childhood

Sarah described her childhood as extraordinarily accomplished, but very strict, but that's not what I recall. I knew her mother was extremely religious and protective, and she was very isolated from the other children in the area.

Her father, though he was a big teddy bear, he had an elaborate set of rules that she had to live by. Sara said the first time she had sex was when she was twenty-five, even though she was engaged on numerous occasions. I find that hard to believe. She told me there was a boy she admired but couldn't say anything, because he was deemed an undesirable or the wrong breed, it was called. I thought her to be exaggerating just a little about her beautiful life because no one who knew the family, could give an account for most of the stuff she was saying. Could it be that a part of her secret was to play the rich kid game.
Maybe, she's trying to fake it till she makes it.

Chapter 3

Sara's First Engagement

Sara said she was engaged for the first time at age fourteen to their preacher's son, but then she broke it off after learning the youth was too jealous. The young man declared he broke it off, after   learning she wasn't a virgin. I understand that the young man was complaining to his father about Sara, who in turn complained to Sara's parents indicating   Sara was too friendly and loved men. They also noted that all of Sara's friends seemed always to be male, and something was troubling about her.

Chapter 4

Sara Got A Job

At age 16, Sara Levy got her first job at a local fried fish and pepper shrimp restaurant, where she met and fell in like with the cook named Barry Royal. They were spending time together, but she claims they never had sex.

The pair were engaged but broke up when the cook caught her with the chicken and shrimp delivery man and claimed they were going together.

On few occasions, the cook saw her going home with the deliveryman sitting on the bar of his bicycle, 'Pedal, and, wheel' style. Sara said she and the cook nor the delivery man, ever had sex. She seems like an ideal girl, **so what could be Sara's secret?**

Chapter 5

Sara's 9th Engagement

Sara was engaged nine more times before she was 18, but she still never walked down the aisle or had sex with any of the men, according to her. She explained all the men accepted her terms of postponing sex until they were married. Sara said she promised her parents; she would not have sex without marriage, and she is keeping her promise.

According to Sara, every man wants to marry her, but she just can't make up her mind. But, was that the case, or is there something else to it. What is Sara's big secret? So many engagements, yet she insists she only had sex with three men in her lifetime.

Is that believable?

Chapter 6

Sara Is Pregnant

At age 25 Sara reconnected with her high school sweetheart in Brooklyn and declared she finally had sex for the first time, and got pregnant.

Sara had already mastered the art of keeping her male friends away from the people who knew her so when it comes down to it, everyone was always in the dark about what Sara actually was doing in the dark.

During her pregnancy and beyond, rumors were swirling that a married Real Estate man, she occasionally was seen with was the actual father of her baby. Sara denied she even had sex with the Real estate man.

There were rumors also that the man believed that the baby was his, but couldn't say anything because he was a married man. Sara denied everything but admitted she did not want any baby at that time and hated being pregnant. She explained that the man jumped her when she wasn't looking and caught her off guard. She said she let him wear a condom in the first session, and she was laying there on her back relaxing and out of nowwhere, he jumped in and discharged inside of her. She said she hated him for that. She certainly was not thrilled about a baby sucking on her breast. She told me she would rather have an ugly man sucking on her breast than a miserable little parasite. Her high school sweetheart, apparently believes her first sexual encounter was with him. For a while he was going around bragging he had taken Sara's virginity.

Chapter 7

Sara's Baby

I think Sara was also worried that the baby may ruin her amazing figure. Again, she was physically a knockout. She was 6 feet tall with a Coca -Cola bottle shape and beauty to kill. Sara also loves to laugh and have fun, and wanted a luxurious lifestyle.

I remember her showing me pictures of a house in Orange County, that she was getting ready to buy. At that time, she was friends with a married High School Principal from up that way who sold her that dream. As soon as he had sex with Sara a few times, he dumped her and shattered her dream of homeownership. Sara arguably stated he is merely a friend.

Sara seems to be loved by every man she meets, but why? What's her secret? There are many beautiful women like her, but they just don't have the same loving - appeal like Sara.

Chapter 8

Fun Girl Sara

Sarah Levy is a woman who loves the easy life, ordering out and room service kind of girl. She spends most of her time pursuing pleasure, and did everything in her power not to work, and to have as little responsiblity as possible. She spends most of her time doing research on men on the Internet and shopping. She told me stories of some of the men she met through the Internet and some stories are just strange. She once had a man who would come around once a week and give her one hundred dollars to suck her toes and leave. She was required to leave her toes as dirty as she could so he'd have a great suck. Sara has the most male friends, and she says she is not having sex with any of them.

So what is Sara's secret?

Chapter 9

Sara's Looks

Sarah's looks have taken her to many high places. She once met a U.S. Senator's driver, while crossing a busy street in Manhattan; they became friends, and she even made it into the Whitehouse on a few occasions. She also appeared at the 19th Grammy Awards Show, when she was friends with a Janitor who works at the Grammy awards building. Sara certainly is not picky and does not date men based on important sounding titles. She is so cool and humble, and men love her. She would date the box boy at the supermarket after breaking up with the manager.

She takes men 'just as they are'. If you run into this beautiful woman, Sara in the street, and think a woman like that would never give herself to you, you may be missing out! You will be disappointed and shocked when you get to know her.

Chapter 10

Is Sara a Woman Of Morals?

Is Sara a woman of high morals? Some speculated that she might be a gold digger who doesn't know how to close the deal and keeps falling in love with her victims. She enjoys wearing the shortest dress at an event, and she is sure to be noticed. She would grab a broom at a wedding if a piece of cake dropped on the floor, just to steal the spotlight. She wants to make sure that everyone leaves talking about the girl in the short dress who was sweeping up the cake.

So why... what's Sara's secret? Why would she feel the need to rush over to mop the floors in her short dress? Maybe, that's what's called true professionalism.

Chapter 11

Sara The Ultimate Daughter In Law

Sarah is not only loved by every man, but she is also adored by every man's mothers and grandmothers. According to Sara, all her male friend's mothers want her as their daughter in law. Every man's mother loves her. Yes, I can see that! She is very easy to talk to and very eager to help and give advice. She would comb grandma's hair to wow the family.

Every man's mother thinks she is wife material. She is especially significant with people handicapped or mentally challenged. She has a natural knack of making people, especially men, feel good.

Chapter 12

Sara Won't Commit Or Separate

Sara doesn't seem to be able to commit to a man or separate from him, similar to how nymphomaniacs usually are. On second thought, she makes commitments all the time but just can't seem to keep them. She would often just change a man's status from a lover to a friend and start referring to her ex as her brethren. She would try to end a relationship, and just couldn't do it, because she always tried to keep the conversation going instead of just ignoring the person. She would call a man and tell him it's over, and in due time, he would get her right back in bed. She sometimes would take a man out to dinner to end a relationship, and instead end up in bed with him for supposedly one last time, and it never ends. Sara couldn't get it in her head that the only way to be rid of a worthless relationship is by ignoring the person.

Chapter 13

Was Sara A Nymphomaniac?

Sarah does show signs of nymphomania, but I can't say for sure at this time. We will soon figure it out. Yes, she certainly appears to have a compulsion to have sex with every man on earth, or at least every man she can get her hands - on. She also never had or seemed capable of having a lasting relationship.

The strange twist here is it seems like she never breaks up with any man; she will leave them temporarily and start addressing them as her brethren. I know of men she formerly dated, and now she says they are now just friends. She would change a man's status if she decided she didn't want to have sex with him anymore.

And by the way, she's never admitted to sleeping with any man besides her baby father. Every man around her is her brethren. Keep reading!!

Chapter 14

Sara The Story Teller

Sarah Levy has told us many big and fantastic stories no one has ever ascertained whether they were true or false. She often speaks about her years working at the famous Uncle Lebanon Hospital, and what a fantastic job she was doing, and how much she was loved. No one can ever doubt how many people loved this woman, but the problem is no one from the hospital knows her.
Is she making up these stories and why?

Once she told me, she invented a baby formula and showed the recipe to someone who stole it and made millions. What could she be covering up?
What is Sara's secret? Could this be just a 'lazy ass woman' who never worked a day in her life and fooling us?
She also told me another big story; it was her mother who invented pumpum shorts, and her friend stole it and made millions.

Yes, I know that anything is possible, but with a girl like Sara, you never know.

Chapter 15

Sara's Curry Chicken

Is Sara's secret in her cooking recipe? Sara often told us stories about her working in a hospital; and one day she made curry chicken, and everyone loved it, and from there, she was required to do it all the time. She said it was the best curry chicken they had ever tasted. Oh really!!

Well, One day, I overheard a conversation between her and one of her sisters, and her sister remarks were that Sara was never the kitchen or cooking type. That statement resonated with me. So, one day, I run into Sara's mother, and mentioned Sara's amazing curry chicken; Her mother told me she's the one who has been cooking curry chicken for Sara; She had no inkling it had anything to do with some hospital. She said her daughter told her she loves curry chicken, and every so often, she would ask her to make a pot for her. Sara takes the pot and pours it out into an aluminum container and puts her name on it.

Chapter 16

Sara's Taxi

Sarah doesn't have a car, neither does she take trains or busses. She views trains and busses as poor folks transportation. This indigent girl, takes so many taxis that some people thought she owned a cab company. More taxis come to her apartment than Grand Central Station.

So, how is she paying all these taxi men? She says all these men are just her good brethrens, and don't mind giving her free rides from the bottom of their hearts.
 If that were true maybe that would explain what I heard; a lot of these taxi men are out there carrying pretty girls around for free and taking none home.

I am not that naive... either they are carrying her for free, or she is paying them with sex. What do you think?
You think these taxi men are carrying her around from the goodness of their heart?

Chapter 17

Sara On The Radio

Sarah met one of Don Sterling's radio photographers, and she ended up as a guest on the show one time. Don did notice her beauty and nice walk, and had her do a little modeling on the set. She was a hit on the show, but not sure why she never went back. The people who knew her were very excited and were hoping to see her on the show again, but it never happened. But why?

I know that Sara is a very busy woman. Every time you see her she's busy, and no one knows what she's busy doing. She is the first woman I know, who doesn't work but is always busy. I assume she has so many men on rotation she can't keep up. She doesn't have time to scratch her head.... like mi granny would say!

Chapter 18

Sara The Movie Star

Sarah always bragged that she played the sexy bartender in the popular film "Dress Naked", but they cut all of her parts, except for one scene in which no one was able to recognize her. She met a bartender friend, at the time they were shooting a movie at the bar where he worked, and he asked his boss to hook her up in a role. Sara is a big movie star, with one exception, no one recognizes her in the movie.

Well, If that's true, why did they cut out her parts? Can she really act? No one knows. Every time she talks about it I tell her to write her bio and go try to get another role. Maybe, she can act, because she always talks about the time spent in drama class at school, and how well she performed.

Chapter 19

Sara The Pig Farmer

Sarah told us she has a big pig farm in Jamaica; She is always describing the pigs and telling pig stories. The problem is, no one in Jamaica knows about Sara's pig farm. I did some checking, and it turns out, one of her so-called brethren's has a little pig farm in Jamaica, and he speaks to her frequently about it. I guess he talks about his pigs so much that

Sara fell in love with the pigs, and began believing she was the owner of the farm; She would describe the various pork parts, and which sections she prefers; from the feet to the lean, spare ribs. LOL. Sara the pork queen!!

Chapter 20

Is Sara A Thief

One day, it was on the news a robbery where someone stole fifty thousand dollars from a police detective, and Sara fits the description. The police was on his way to headquarters to drop off the money and stopped and picked up a friend to get a blowjob. In the middle of the blowjob, the lady transfers the money to her pocket book without the detective feeling anything.

For months everyone wondered if it was Sara because right after the robbery, she came home wearing fifteen hundred dollars shoes; she also didn't leave her apartment for two weeks.

Anyway, about seven months later they catch the thief and it was not Sara.

Chapter 21

Sara On TV

Sarah was seen on television for the first time when she was a guest in the audience on the Jerry Springer show. That was a big buzz for Sara, and yes, she represented! The topic was, 'sleeping with your best friends, man'.

Not to judge, but, it seems like Sara was comfortable with the matter. I find it fascinating because people always wondered about Sara; how does she have the galls to do something like that. Sara is a very amiable woman... to every man; don't know if she even has any principles or standards when it comes to men!

Anyway, Jerry went over to her with the mic, and Sara got up and said, "I don't understand why women would battle over men, and men are sufficient out there; even if I have to share I don't care". Sara said it with such an attitude, and the people respond hugely; Sara received the biggest applause on the show that day.

Chapter 22

Sara And The Married Men

In 2001, Sara began dating a married Real Estate broker... The people who know her, say that's a regular thing for Sara, but Sara says it never happened before.

Anyway, the man said something she didn't like one day, so she began dating one of his agents who had a prior interest. The man said it was just a simple joke; he never thought she would take it so hard. All he said to her was; "Go home". They were hanging out in his office, and he was ready to leave, and she didn't want to go, and he said Go home, and she had a fit and stormed off. I think Sara is unable to tolerate nonacceptance.

Anyway, it caused a big riff in the office. The boss ended up firing the agent, and the agent sued and subpoenaed Sara to testify, and the boss settled with the agent.

So, what is Sara's secret? Why is she searching?

What is she lacking? Why does she continuously jump from man to man? Does she even have an inkling as to what she wants? Is she communicating her needs? What is her approach?

Just keep reading!!

Chapter 23

The Old Man With The Deal

Sara met a 70- year - old ex - soldier named Nathan, and they became friends. Shortly after, she borrowed money from Nathan to help pay her rent. She told him she would pay him back in three weeks but didn't, but Nathan told her to keep it because he loved her. Nathan doesn't have any money but he recieves an Army pension.

Three months later, Sara borrowed money from him again, but this time he proposed that she could borrow some cash and pay down on a cheap house up north, where both of them and her kids could live together until his death, and she inherits the house. Sara needed more money than is necessary to go to the supermarket, so she said yes.

Yes, Sara would accept that proposal from a one foot man rather than fall behind on her bills. Nathan was so excited, he jumped into gear and started shopping for loans and houses, and two weeks later he called Sara with some good news. Nathan found an old house in Rochester, and was approved for a mortgage, and wanted he and Sara to go look at it, but that was the last time he heard from Sara.

Chapter 24

Sara Turns To Jesus

In 2002, Sara turned to Jesus. Sara joined a church in Brooklyn after meeting the Reverend at a produce store. The Reverend was picking up several bottles of Olive Oil on sale, and Sara asked him if he could pass her a bottle of Curry which was right beside the Olive Oil. The Reverend began talking to her about 'this man' he knew and wanted to introduce Sara to him. He assured Sara, this man's father is prosperous and has a big mansion paved with Gold and all sorts of goodies. Sara couldn't resist meeting this man and was in church promptly the following Sunday. To the surprise of the other parishioners, Reverend made Sara an usher her second Sunday.

Everyone was upset after noticing her closeness with the Reverend and suddenly she was handling his money. The Reverend even started mentoring Sara and promoted her to substitute preacher. The other women in the church were dismayed but Sara's reign didn't last long. The Reverend turned away from her after noticing the church van driver was giving her charity rides all over the place.

There was the gossip she was dating the Reverend and the church van driver at the same time.
So why? Is this a woman who needs a different man for every occasion? Maybe, she sees herself as the Queen, and all the men are her subjects.

Remember that one of the first men she cheated with was taking her home on the bicycle bar.
Maybe, Sara's secret is she's trying to find a different man to fill every opening she has.

She once told me about a notion to host an annual male only barbecue, where she'd have all her male friends working the grills and serving her.

Could it be that the only secret here is that Sara just loves men?

Chapter 25

Sara The Politician

In 2003, Sara went into politics; she ended up on the NYC Mayoral election team, Traveling around with the election committee, hanging out at campaign meetings, and big hotels for free.

Sara's parents especially were ecstatic but were concerned if she were doing it for business or just to meet men? Well, she once told me about the enormous business plans and ideas she had to open an Adult Care Center; she said, someone, promised her if the Mayor won, they were going to cite her, but after the election, we heard nothing more about those plans.

One thing, I know, any Mayor who has Sara on his side will gain a victory. Sara merely has a way with people. She can get anyone to do anything if she sets her mind to it, but the question is, is she working her game right? Up until now, she still has nothing but her killer looks and body.

Chapter 26

Sara's Lessons

What is the lesson here, or is there even one? Does Sara explain the expression, 'beauty is only skin deep', or 'you can't judge a book by the cover'? You will find out shortly, but I have to mull over it myself, and give my thoughts concerning this beauty.

The first time I saw her, I remember seeing an influential woman whom I didn't know, but that's what I saw. Could it be she doesn't see herself the way people discern her, or maybe as a child no one told her how stunning she was. It is also quite possible they were telling her the opposite; where I'm from that is a tremendous problem. People occasionally speak erroneously to children and cause chaos in their life.

Chapter 27

Is Sara Mentally Ill

Sarah doesn't like keeping women friends because they gossip too much, and that they are usually envious of her. She said every time she tries having a female friend, her man often becomes fond of them, and her friends can't deal with the attention.

She once told me the story about being evicted from her apartment, and her friend allowed her to stay with her for few weeks then accused her of sleeping with her husband. Sara denied it, of course, but no one who knows her would put it pass Sara.

We know by now, Sara certainly knows how to tell the untruth; she is also very barefaced and dry - eyed. I believe all the pride and shame she has doesn't apply when it comes to men.

Maybe, Sara's big secret is that she loves sleeping with people's men.

Chapter 28

It's Money Story Time Again

Sarah told me so many fantastic money stories; I can hardly keep up; she oversees all this money but has none. Maybe, she is just too honest. I recall her mentioning her friend gave her one hundred and fifty thousand dollars to put in the bank for him. I said, wow! You have wealthy friends!

Another time, I recall her telling me about her brethren, the party promoter, who would often time put her at the gate to collect his money, and she would receive thousands and deliver it all to him. I don't get it. In reality, she has no money! Was she telling us money stories like some of her males were doing to her? Maybe, she spends so much time with different men; she began to adapt their ways.

Most men tend to act like they have money. She shared the time she was in a car accident and had a case pending and often talks about all the settlement payments they turned down. At one point, they were offering her two hundred fifty thousand, and her lawyer advised her to turn it down because he was confident they could get more.

Anyway, she told these stories for a while until they go away, and she remains broke. Was Sara just a victim who fell in love with her abusers, and became like them?

Chapter 29

So What is Sara's Secret?

Did Sara attend College? Sara often spoke about her essential college days at New York University, but I never talked to anyone who went to that college during that time period who'd ever heard of her. I've never met one of her college buddies. Could it be that she made up all these stories just to look good?

After all, this is a professional woman who was never seen going to work. What is a professional woman anyway? Some hookers do refer to themselves as professionals or working girls, and who can blame them. Having sex with a bunch of strangers, I would imagine a tough endeavor. I am not saying, Sara is a hooker, I just don't know how she earns her money; that's all.

And even if she is a hooker, it's honest labor.
So, how does Sara make her money? What is Sara's secret?

Chapter 30

Sara The Nurse

Sarah Levy said she'd had numerous careers, including CNA, in a major hospital, but I've never seen her go to work. She spoke of how the men loved her because of the outstanding job she was doing, and how the jealous women despised her. She said the top executives gave her unlimited access, and the other females didn't appreciate it. They accused her of doing sexual favors for the bosses and getting special treatment; due to budget cuts, she was laid off and collected unemployment.

What is Sara's secret; could it be she likes having sex in risky places? She's known to have had sexual encounters a few times, in parks, on the roadsides, etc.; She often said whenever she meets the man of her dreams, she will have lovemaking with him everywhere. She says she often dreams of having a man, and walking into his office, and pushing his computer to the side, open up and let him take her right on the desk. Well, it's very possible she was caught having sex at the hospital and was terminated...

Who knows? All I know is I would love to be a fly on the wall anywhere she working to see the impression on the other women's faces. It appears she thinks every man belongs to her, and she always goes overboard trying to impress.

Chapter 31

Sara's Pride

Sarah is an excessively proud woman from a very dignified Jamaican family, and as they say, "Pride comes before a fall". I would declare she is honorable way beyond the normal, but was that the enigma to why she never stayed long - on anything? Some say she remained slender over the years because she wouldn't ask for food; even if starvation were killing her, pride wouldn't allow her to tell a man she's hungry.

She would often share stories with me about her dates, and they never involved eating or going out to dinner. I never heard her say a man cooked for her or took her out to eat. Every man in her life seems just only to take her to bed, and most importantly, she would spend all day in bed and not eat.

I recall Valentine's Day, I picked her up a plate of food, and she still talks about it up to this day; perhaps, It was the first time a man ever paid for her food.
My heart goes out to Sara; because I believe no one has ever taught this little girl how to survive.

Chapter 32

It Is Better To Give Than To Receive

It's hard to imagine how a girl like Sara doesn't have anything; taking into account my history with women, I don't get it.
The secret here may be a religious one.
Sara does have a deep religious family background, and one of the lessons they taught in church is,
"it's better to give than to receive".

Could Sara's secret have to do with severe religious vitriol? Some people take their church teaching very literally and seriously. They believe the more they give, the more Jesus will love them, and higher is the prospect of getting a room in his Mansion. Come to think of it; 'giving is receiving'. So, Sara probably feels that when she's having sex, she is both giving and receiving at the same time, which means she is fulfilling her religious obligation with God. Maybe, she feels every man she has sex with is similar to missionary work.

Chapter 33

Sara's Self-Esteem

Based on what I observed, I don't think Sara has any self-esteem at all. The telltale sign is she can't implore men for money, and she's eager to please everyone just for praise. Women who think highly of themselves are not shy about asking for things.

Sara, on the other hand, loves to influence men. If a plumber comes to fix her pipe, she is the plumber's assistant. If the cable guy arrives, she's helping him.

Once two painters were painting her apartment, and she grabbed a brush and helped them paint in her short tight up skirt. Sara was in all her glory. LOL.
What do you make of that?

Chapter 34

Sara's Bed Bugs

One day, one of Sara's male friends caught bed bugs on Sara's bed and told people in the building. Sara took it badly because once people got a whiff, the building's top model has bed bugs, they teased, cursed, and embarrassed her terribly. Sara fled the apartment for one month leaving the keys with the super to take care of the problem. She and the super were extremely tight, and other residents argued the super is spending too much time in Sara's apartment.

One thing I know is that Sara has so much Pride, having bed bugs is the very last scandal she wanted.

Yep, removing bed bugs these days is a big event.
Anyway, that too was past, and Sara still has her secret.

Chapter 35

Was Sara An Abused Child?

Sarah could have been an abused child and never discussed it. I raised the question and, she said no; but for me, she exhibits more victim than the abuser. The offensive capability I see with Sara is sleeping with men other than her own with irrational contentment. She comes across as enjoying functioning as a sex offender as if she is accustom to it.

She is very at home sneaking around; Sara would take a man if his woman turned her attention for five minutes. I suspect that she was sexually assaulted by someone who was in a relationship with someone extremely close to her; could even be a stepfather!

Read on!!

Chapter 36

Why Sara Changes Men So Often?

Sarah has multiple men who desire her, but they can't maintain her for long. For me, I suspect it could have something to do with hunger the reason she changes men so frequently. I believe that if she was assaulted sexually as a youth, her abusers were someone who was providing food for her.

Maybe, she is searching for that father figure who would ask, 'is my little girl hungry?'. If she never had to ask for food growing up, she might not be capable of doing it.
So, was Sara searching for another father?
 That could very well be Sara's big mystery.

Chapter 37

Was Sara On Public Assistant?

I surmise Sara is the kind of woman who would instead find a secret older man to support her than to stand - in the Welfare line.

Yes, like I said before, she has the most extreme arrogance; I've ever come across, and I think she is the type of girl who would prefer to go hungry rather than to stand - in the Welfare line.

Arrogance could be one of the reasons she has multiple male friends; they are like her barrier to keep things intact around her. Sara never wants any of the men around her to be her enemy; she would go above and beyond for the men closest to her. The men closest to her could run an off - color joke, and she would overlook it, and if a man from the outside made that same joke, she wouldn't tolerate it. There is a metaphor that says; you shouldn't crap where you sleep because you then will have to lie in it. If you're messing around with the folks you have to see everyday, then you have to take all their crap.

Chapter 38

Sara Met Sports Tycoon

In 2005, Sara Levy met Canada's sports tycoon Melvin Howell II, while helping out her friend serving hot dogs at a food stand at his stadium. Mr. Howell was passing by and Sara caught his eye and he began asking: 'who is that girl?', and eventually someone brought Sara in to meet him.

So, here was Sara, meeting probably the richest man in the stadium, and she made nothing of it. She is still penniless and telling big money stories. She boasted about being invited to his penthouse, and they became best of friends, and remain so up until this day; I understand this to be credible because she always gets a bunch of tickets to his big hockey games.

Back to reality, because the only thing she seems to gain from this rich man is some free tickets to his games and a few memorabilia to impress the men in her life who enjoy hockey.

Chapter 39

Does Every Man Really Love Sara

Yes, knowing Sara, I would go out on a limb and say, with her sexy image, Sara Levy, is every man's love at first sight. People seem to have an insatiable interest in this bubbly, curvaceous girl, who can work her stuff, very much like Marilyn Monroe. She tries to be so modest about it, but I know she loves the attention she got from everyday men, and she's not picky about who she's getting it from. She loves to smile and take pictures, and she has thousands of them. She loves attention, and she often flirts like a queen or a diva, referring to men as her boys, while playing naive, pretending to be stunned, when I mentioned how loved she was.

Chapter 40

What Does Sara Want?

Sarah looks like she has everything until you learn the truth. She manages to project a wealthy woman's image with nothing but her looks. I guess what they say is true: 'Image is everything'.

The question many ask is, why? Why is Sara searching? Is this a woman who craves and loves sex?
Despite all her big wealthy friends, she still lives below modest in a tiny basement apartment.

What is this girl searching for, no one knows?

I still haven't figured out where she is actually driving to, or what she is going after. Stay focused!!

Chapter 41

Sara And Married Men

I noticed that Sara loves having Married male friends, but when I asked why all she did was laugh, and she said they are less work.

Yes, I get that; having a relationship with a married man means Sara doesn't have to wash, cook, clean, or keep house for him, and I know that Sara is not interested in doing any of that stuff. Nonetheless, she was in a committed relationship with a married man and loved it; she said, she was faithful to this married man, I hadn't thought it possible for any woman to be that committed to a married man, but, maybe, Sara did it.

Maybe, that was Sara's big secret...
Is she sleeping with every married man in the building. She figured if she were committed to a married man she wouldn't have to do anything for him.

Chapter 42

Sara's Dysfunction

Sarah just happens to know a lot about sexual dysfunction, but how come she knows so much about that stuff? Maybe, that's just how it is when a young girl dates old broken down grandpas. I noticed Sara always inquired as to how to help men with sexual problems.

One time she asked me if I knew what men in Jamaica use to enhance their sex drive? Sara was trying to become an expert in sexual malfunction. Maybe, she developed sympathy for older men when they gave her money, and she's trying to provide them with a little sex, and they can't get it up.

One day, I saw an older man stop by to drop off a package to her, and I thought he was the original prune face. I think damn! Where does she find these men... probably on the Internet wearing their make up.

Chapter 43

Meet The Parents

Sara's parents are retired and moved back to Jamaica to live, and only visit her once in a while. Of course, she always talks about them and sharing her great childhood stories with me. Sara told me that the father she always spoke about is her stepfather and that she wasn't acquainted with her birth father until she was an adult. She explained her stepfather is her birth father, and her birth father was just her sperm donor.

One day, she told me her parents were coming for two weeks and pleaded with me to pick them up at the airport. That day we went to Kennedy Airport to pick them up and I saw her stepfather, he and Sara look and act exactly alike. I couldn't get over it! This is a big mystery to me.
If you didn't know them and saw them walking together, you would have to ask if they are father and daughter. I inquired on many occasions if she were sure he wasn't her actual father, and she replied, "she was confident. " And, yes! Up until this day, I will never every buy that! Something just doesn't add up to me.

Chapter 44

Is Sara Doing What She Really Likes?

I believe Sara hates working and doing homework, and I never hardly see her doing any of that; so, I have to say she must be doing what she likes.
Once in a while, I would see her pushing her laundry cart to the laundry room and that's about it.

Another thing I know she likes is shopping, and she's always doing that; shopping and going on outings and on dates are some of Sara's favorite things. She would just call one of her brethren and send him to the supermarket to get her flavored bottle water. She's got it like that. She is also fortunate to find male friends who can persuade their Auntie to watch her son every time she has to go away.

Chapter 45

Sara's Oldest Lover, Maybe:

At age 27, Sara Levy met a 78 - year - old man and started spending a lot of time with him. He was not wealthy, but she said he has a nice pension. No one ever saw her with the man. I was the only person she allowed to meet him. Maybe, she was ashamed to be seen with him because of the tremendous age difference. Anyway, the old man did not complain. She made him a sweet deal if he stayed out of sight; he would be rewarded. No one could tell she was after his money, because he wasn't a wealthy man, but Sara was satisfied knowing he had just enough to pay her rent and a few dollars more.
With Mr. pension paying her rent, she was able to continue her mysterious star girl, play girl image. Mr. pension also got his apartment decorated to suit Sara, so she feels at home when she visits. She got seven - years from Mr. pension until he passed away.

Chapter 46

The Sara's Old Men Show:

In 2012, Sara had an idea and started a fashion shows for older men. The Sara Levy Show's purpose was to scout for older men with money, build up their confidence and teach them how to go after hot girls. The basis for the show is older men dressing their best, and walking on the runway. She would have them do it and counsel them to build - up their confidence .

In my view, she was just searching for another older man to pay her rent. The show didn't really jump off because, she wanted her sports tycoon friend to sponsor it and he refused. Maybe, he was jealous and thought he might lose his place. Sara is always very sympathetic to men. She understands them, she knows how to talk to them no matter age, race or deformity. She would date a one-foot man with a pension. I forgot to ask her how old her father was. Maybe, she was 'old man picking'! She was often seen in the company of older men, homeless men, sick men, any men... all kinds of men.

Chapter 47

Sara With No Sugar Daddy

Sarah tuned 39 and found herself with no poor older man paying her rent, and she is depressed. Sara was a woman without a career, calling herself a professional woman. She was able to do that by finding a fool to pay her rent and be quiet about it. Now she doesn't have a sugar daddy and she is like a fish out of water. Imagine, if she is behind on her rent and they start an eviction; that would be suicidal for Sara, with her pride, she couldn't handle it. She promoted herself as a professional career woman who was living the high life without working or having a care in the world. Sara was able to live that way, thanks to an older man somewhere. Maybe, her secret is in her "old man plan".

Chapter 48

Sara's Fist Fight

Sarah Levy found herself in the middle of an altercation with a friend and neighbor who accused her of having an affair with her husband. The argument turns ugly when the lady slaps Sara in the face, and Sara just ignores the hit, and keeps walking calmly away like nothing happened. Everyone was saying mmmmm!! yet shocked at how calmly Sara handled the accusations. Sara's friend, a photographer, who lived in the same building, took some pictures of the incident and posted them on FB. Everyone was in disbelief and couldn't understand why Sara took the hit and walked away. Some speculated that the accusations must have been right, and Sara just tried to avoid anything else further being revealed. Knowing Sara more than anyone, my take is that the man is an asset and Sara needs him for something. Maybe, he is one man who gives without Sara asking. When Sara finds a man like that she cherishes him.

Chapter 49

Sara's Baby

Out of Sara's many engagements, she did bear a son for a man ten years younger than her who she called her high school sweetheart. She probably just thinks the name: 'high school sweetheart' makes her look chic and important.

Many people believe the kid is not his, because he looks more like one of Sara's older brethren who is a real estate agent. The child's father hears the rumors too, and starts asking questions, but, Sara took him out to a fast food, chicken and fish restaurant and he never questioned it again.

Chapter 50

Sara's Body

Sarah was always very strict and secure about what goes into that beautiful body of hers. When she is on dates, she hardly eats. Maybe, a person can live on love after all!! Either that or Sara was just shy or too cute to ask for food. Sara also doesn't take too many risks in the bedroom. She doesn't practice having sex without condoms, and she never accepted a drink from any man unless it came in a twist off bottle cap. She was very protective of her body.

Chapter 51

Sara's Taste In Music

Sarah enjoys sensual, sexy music. She is a very sensual woman. She loves to feel loved. With the right man and the right music, there's nothing she loves more than lying on that man's chest all day, doing nothing but making love and thinking of nothing else. She adores a man who has the time to just lie their all day making love with her and touching her face. Maybe, that's why she always shows interest in older retired men. They tend to have more time.

Is that Sara's secret? Older retired men who don't have to get up and go to work. Maybe she is terrified of being alone.

Chapter 52

Sara's Public Image

In public, Sara treats all men like they are just friends. If she run into the man she spent the night with she would say: "hi, long time no see" just to throw people off. Sara treats every man the same when she is in public. On the street, every man she sees is her brethren, so you cannot discern who she's sleeping with, and the men always just go along. The men know if they play along, they have some good sex coming down the road. There was always speculation regarding her relationship with the men around her. She has the same disposure with every man.

How does she do it? Maybe, she is a high functioning mentally ill woman after all. I would think it would take multiple personalities to pull that off. Is that Sara's secret?

Chapter 53

Sara's Wedding

Was Sara a married woman under quiet? Some speculated that she was secretly married to an older man with a pension, and no one knew. Was that Sara's secret? It was always a mystery as to how Sara's rent got paid. Someone was giving her just enough money to eat, buy clothes and pay her rent, and no one quite sure who it was.

After her first rent check died, she was still eating and still is without job, but I guess was not without sin. Yes, I believe Sara was awesome enough to get any older man to do things exactly the way she wanted to stay in her good graces. Yes, Sara told me she was never married but, I honestly don't believe her. Keep reading!

Chapter 54

Sara's Craves

Is Sara just a girl who is trying to please everyone? She likes to be praised and she craves attention. She also seems to crave validation, belongingness and recognition. Maybe, it makes her think and feel complete. Maybe, it makes her feel whole. It probably makes her feels accomplished also. I believe its because she is an irresponsible person. She doesn't like working or doing anything, so she just makes up things to make herself look good. Yes, Sara definitely loves attention. She just cannot get enough.

Chapter 55

Is Sara In An Interracial Relationship

One day out of nowhere, Sara just came out and said she doesn't date white men. I was so shocked because she doesn't strike me as a woman who would have a problem dating a white man. I was stunned when she told me that, not sure why she felt the need to share with me. She came from a strong religious background, and I never seen any Jamaican from that background who would have a problem dating white. It was extremely unusual. I don't know why she would say that I know it's not right because I know her better than that. Something just doesn't add up, and I simply don't know what it is. I asked her why, and she said it's because she doesn't love the way they smell. Very strange conversation!!

Chapter 56

Is Sara Afraid To Be Alone?

Is Sara afraid to be alone? Everywhere Sara goes, She meets a man, literally!! She loves it when men tell her a success or money story. She would often call me to share her most recent discussion / story a man just told her. And yes, some of the stories men tell her are nothing but made up bullshit. She would meet a man, and he would just make up a sweet money story to say to her and earn her friendship; they know she's looking for something, and they are always feeding her. Sara seems to believe everything men tell her.

Chapter 57

Is It A Dirty Little Secret

What could be so serious about Sara's secret? This secret is not making Sara any money. She doesn't smoke or drink. I know she not involved in selling drugs or in any illegal activities. What is it she trying so hard to conceal from everyone?

She once shared with me that one of her girlfriends died during a rough sex session with her sugar daddy. She explained, her friend was dating an older man who told her he is turned on by choking. She mumbled, the man asked her to choke him, and then he started choking her, and she ended up dead; she also said she was in the house when it occurred, so, maybe, she is traumatized by that. I thought, how come she know all the details about the incident, and dead women tell no tales, then she admitted that she was there? What do you think?

Chapter 58

Sara's Ambition

Sarah always said she met many people who encourage her to pursue modeling, but she was just too reticent. I know her pride kept her from doing many things, but I didn't think she was the quiet type. She and someone once started a home based dressmaking business, but her partner dropped her after noticing that she only wanted to plop in bed all day with men. She always has enormous ideas, and she would start something but never stays focused on accomplishing anything. It appears that one of her problems is her inability to say no to a man.

When she started the dressmaking business, one day her partner came on the street looking for her, explaining they had plans to go to the fabric store and she's not answering her phone. I knew why she wasn't answering but I didn't say anything; yes, she was in there with a man.

Chapter 59

The Sara Fascination

Sarah Levy continues to be a subject of great fascination and speculation to this day. She is a real mystery woman who just intrigues everyone. Once you talk to her, she gets in your head and stays there. She still has her calm, high wacky persona with an extra loud laugh here and there. She tends to overreact sometimes, but everyone always gravitated to her style and taste. Men love her and women fear her. She tries out all the things that relate to easy money but never was able to close the deal.

She tried church, politics, acting, sex, singing, etc., but never made any money. So what was Sara's secret? Could it be that she was looking for what was free under the son, or the Sun?

Chapter 60

Is Sara Just A Sex Toy

It appears to me that no one believes Sara is good for anything besides sex, including Sara. She gets picked up by luxury cars, flying out for days or weeks sometimes; then, she would come back home penniless, and nothing changes in her economics. She doesn't have a car of her own, or even a driver's license. She told me over and over again that she doesn't like to ask men for cash. I tried to counsel her, but, I guess it's hard to bend a tree when it's grown... That would explain why she's always hanging with the rich and famous, and she has nothing of her own. She has a lot of groupie tendencies except that most groupies will make sure they are paid.

Chapter 61

Did God Save This Queen

Sarah's big secret and what Sara was searching for, only God knows so far! Sara cannot save herself. She is now 45 and has never been destitute like this before. She is also unhappy and troubled. However, she still looks pretty good. She now has a little belly and a little sag sag here and there, but she is still a pretty awesome catch. Yes, nature was very kind to this woman. She is the definition of "blessed and highly favored".

Chapter 62

Sara A Falling Woman

I heard the term falling woman before but wasn't quite sure what it meant until Sara. Sara is falling down and apart literally. Even her laugh has gotten smaller. Yes, Sara is now falling fast and who is going to catch her, or is anyone going to try to catch her... or is the right person going to catch her?

Suppose no one catches her, what will happen to Sara?!!!! Who is going to even want to catch Sara when she really needs help. It will take someone special. My grandma use to speak of falling women as they were prostitutes.

I remember one night, a prostitute came to church, and the church caught on fire. Everyone was trying to save that woman's soul for Jesus. Of course, I was too young to know who she was at the time, but I remember after church mama was talking about the falling woman. Some years later, I learned what a falling woman does and went and experienced one. She was nice!!

Chapter 63

Sara Met A Man Name Joshua

Then one day, at age 45, Sara met a man named Joshua, who saw something in her that no other man or even Sara herself could see, but was it too late? Joshua approached Sara from a honesty and truth perspective, but by now, Sara may be already lost. She may have already accepted her role as a sexually assaulted PLAYGIRL, who got played so much, she became familiar, and fell in love with her abusers, and doesn't know anything else. Sara and Joshua's relationship has gotten intense at times as Sara started calling Joshua's honesty, disrespectful. She would be upset with Joshua for days and wouldn't speak to him. Why was she so upset with Joshua... did Joshua figure out her secret?

The one thing unique about this relationship is that Sara always wants to hear everything Joshua is saying. She disagrees with him all the time and declared he doesn't understand her, but she remains intrigued with every utterance from Joshua's mouth.

Can Joshua save Sara?; would he even try to snag her?

Chapter 64

Sara's Counselor

Joshua tried to counsel and educate Sara to be more responsible and stop trying to pursue a life of pleasure without responsibility or attachments. Joshua explains that there's nothing free under the sun, but Joshua's truth continues to be too harsh for Sara to cope with. Sara would be so irritated with Joshua at times, but it appears she was acquiring an infatuation with Joshua. Sara was still desperately trying to maintain her Playgirl diva role, laughing big on the outside and still trying to satisfy every man, but Joshua's words keep getting in her way.

Chapter 65

Sara Stabs Joshua

One day, Joshua was standing outside, and a Mercedes Benz came to pick Sara up; the man returned her the next day. Joshua told Sara he wanted to converse with her, and she invited him over.

The following day, Joshua went over to Sara's place and spoke to her harshly about changing her ways, and the conversation got hot, and Sara became flippant and stabbed Joshua in his shoulder with a fountain pen. Sara was so hysterical; she called the police, who arrested Joshua. She said Joshua has no right to speak to her like that because he is not paying her bills.

Chapter 66

Sara's Suicide Attempt

The following week, after the Joshua incident, everyone was stunned when an ambulance came and carried Sara away. Sara was inaccessible, causing her superintendent to be intrusive, finding her very overdosed. Sara was whisked away and got treatment and some counseling returning home several days later.

As for me, I still cannot believe it; and I learned a vital lesson that day. Sara was the very last person I thought would attempt to take her life. Shortly after, Sara is back on her feet again and ready for more action.

Chapter 67

Sara In The Studio

After the recovery, Sara met a small time music producer who convinced her she had musical talents. They went into a relationship and he recorded a song with Sara. Everyone who hears the song laughed at her and said she couldn't sing. She was heartbroken and broke off her relationship with the producer. She told me she just stopped talking to him and plans never to speak to him again.

Chapter 68

Did Sara Become Joshua?

Joshua became known and recognized as Sara's significant influence. Sara's savior, if you will!! Sara began to sound like Joshua and folks noticed. Sara was so different than the people around were accustomed to; they began calling her Joshua.

She got funnier and even began using some of Joshua's teachings on others. We heard the term: "other half" or "better half", I am confident one of those terms fits in this story somewhere. These two people were made for each other.

Chapter 69

Sara Back With Baby Father

After this Sara decided to lay low for few weeks, get back with her baby father. She brought him in to live with her in the basement. For now, no more trips or luxury car pickups for almost a year. During this time she barely came outside the apartment. The baby father was paying the rent and going to the market for her, and she would spend most of her time inside. I think she was a little embarrassed to be seen with the baby father because he wasn't really a statuette man. She eventually gave her baby father his walking papers, and was back by herself for a week before she got lonely again.

Chapter 70

Can Joshua Save The Queen?

One week after breaking up with the baby father, Sara called Joshua, and they kiss and make up. She didn't apologize with words, but Joshua enjoyed her method of apology. She even gave Joshua a blowjob, and told him it was the first time she gave a man a blowjob. Yes, I question her about her first blowjob claim, and I happened to believe her. Sara's not into too much foreplay, she just wants her insertion right away.

So, Can Joshua save the Queen? What Joshua was saying to Sara has resonated and made her think, which may have triggered the stabbing.
The truth hurts, like they say.

Joshua made her a deal if she stays out of trouble for two years; he will marry her and save her. The deal was he would have to get rid of all the men who have manipulated her for sex, and become loyal to him before he espouses her. In my opinion, if it's true that Joshua's knob was the first she polished, I would say she found true love. **What do you think of Joshua?**

Chapter 71

Is Sara's Vagina More Sweet or Free?

Was Sara vagina that good or is it any complimentary vagina is always favorable; same as said about free liquor.

It seems like Sara has a set of men who would miss her ever so often, and would go in search of Sara. Some she only saw once a year while others, on a case by case basis over a long period of time.

These guys had it good for a long time; then one day Joshua came and messed things up for them. A part of the deal Joshua made Sara was to change her number and stop answering all strange numbers.

Soon after, reality struck these guys who realized, they can no longer reach their free punany. Every so often, a strange man would show up on her street poking around for her, claiming he worried and wanted to see if she was ok. It went on like that for two years. As soon as one of her men wanted some free vagina and couldn't reach her, they would circle around the block praying for a stroke of good luck.

Chapter 72

Sara Moves Away

Finally, after two years, Joshua decided to move Sara away to the Caribbean Island, St. Kitts. They arrive in St. Kitts among new people, new atmosphere, new attitude, and a much stronger Sara. Sara told me moving was the happiest thing she's ever done. She said she has been looking for an escape for years and moving was it. So what's the message here!
Read on!!

Chapter 73

What Was Sara's #1 Secret?

It turned out that Sara was so popular and loved because of this one fault she had, she never asked for money or favors from the men prior to sex. Those bastards loved her for that. She'd instead go hungry or borrow money from her brother or parents, rather than to ask the man she just spent the night pleasuring; for one dollar. Sara did have friends she would call and hint she may need cash, and they would volunteer. Those guys were not statuette but would steal for Sara, but she never acknowledged them as even her friends.

Secret #2 coming up!!

Chapter 74

How Does A Fool Start Over

After a rollercoaster ride with so many different men, and after so many men became accustomed to Sara's kindness, Sara has learned that when you make the mistake of initiating   being everyone's fool, you may have to move to a brand new location physically, and start all over again to fix that problem.

It is not simple to reteach people after you've already taught them; and Sara found that out, that's why she contemplated suicide as the only way out.
Thanks to Joshua, he actually saves Sara.

Chapter 75

Happiness For Sara At Last

SAfter the move, Sara's letter to Joshua. Hi Dear, I never knew love like this before!!

You are my savior. Thank you for saving me. I never imagined I would see the day when my life would be no longer about my pretty looks and sex. Thank you for loving me for me. Your excessive understanding and care gave me a feeling of heavenly love and happiness. You fill me with more joy and peace than I could have ever imagined. Last night, when I was lying next to you, snuggled up close, my head on your chest, I listened to your heartbeat, and I was overwhelmed by a wave of emotions. I beg God to keep you safe because if you were ever to leave me, I don't know how I would carry on. When you slide out of bed and take your warmth away, I don't feel the same. I could never have hoped to have felt like this. When you hold me in your arms with that gentle power, I feel so safe and secure! I cannot be more thankful to you for saving me.

Our journey has been beautiful and steady, and I love you each day even more than the day before.

You love and took me for who I am, and I am forever grateful to have such a wonderful Husband! This is the happiest time of my life! It takes a real man to love me like you do. To love me despite my condition; on my good days and bad days... Thank you for saving me! I love you with all my heart!

Chapter 76

So What Was Sara's #1 Secret?

Sarah is a nymphomaniac!! It's a bit complicated, but, she finally came clean with Joshua. Yes, Sara is a very attractive woman who just wants to have sex everyday. Yes, Sara is a nymphomaniac, and she felt she should make a living from the oldest profession, but didn't know how to work the money part. She is not a streetwalker but her plan was to exchange sex for money, but just couldn't figure out how to handle her account receivables. She told me she tried and tried, and practiced, but every time she tried asking for money she chickened out. Sara doesn't wear a call girl or a hookers uniform, but that's what she is at heart. I heard there was once a Queen from our past who was just like Sara; she had that same type of secret Sara had. She was a nymphomaniac, wearing Royal garments, and like they say: "The Clothes Makes The Man". If a singer dresses like a streetwalker, what is she? Well, I have to say she sells both music and sex.

Yes, my readers!

Our very own sweet, beautiful, sexy, wonderful and amazing Sara, is A Nymphomaniac. She has a neurotic condition in which the symptoms are a compulsion to have sexual intercourse with as many men as possible, and an inability to have lasting relationships with them. Sara's sexual obsession bothers her. She feels guilty after every encounter, but she just can't stop.

Chapter 77

Is Sara Still All Play and No Work?

It turns out that Sara had some good ideas that she never pursued because she was busy giving and receiving sex on top of sex. Well, finally, now that she has a no - nonsense man in her life, Sara has begun to pursue some of her ideas.

How should Joshua handle this relationship?

Well, for me, I would watch Sara like a Hawk, until I am sure she won't relapse?

In the meantime, Sara is a much stronger woman. Sara's self-esteem has gotten a big boost. She is no more a pushover, and she is on treatment to help her condition.

Chapter 78

Conclusion

Well, we have learned that it's easier to move physically and start over from scratch than to retrain the people that you already trained to use and abuse you. We learned that the one who really loves you, will tell you the truth when the truth is needed to save you. It is really the truth that saved Sara, so, it is true like they say: "Only the truth shall set you free". Sara knows the truth, and so she certainly knows who's mouth the truth was coming from, and that was Joshua. She tried to shut Joshua up because she couldn't handle the truth, but the truth turned out to be the most powerful force here, which means the cure to fix every problem on earth the right way, can be found in the truth.

Like in Sara's case the truth was exceedingly terrible, in her eyes, she would rather die than let it come out. She felt she would not be accepted as a normal woman if people knew she was a Nymphomaniac, but she didn't realize, that was the reason so many people loved her. Maybe, nymphomaniacs have some amazing qualities no one else has!!

Anyway, when Joshua came along and told Sara he loved her regardless, that must have caused Sara to see herself a little differently. Joshua had no problem with Sara's nymphomania. He was more exasperated that she wasn't using intercourse to take these bastards money, allowing them to use her, which they found amusing. You have to teach the people around you how to treat you, and if you have taught them that you're giving away free pumpum, once they get the first taste of your freedom, they are not going to pay for it.

Yep, it may be easier to move away than to muster up all the strength and courage, and time needed to re-teach, and reteach every one of those people the new you. Moving away and Starting over is not easy and can give you a dreadful feeling, but it isn't as hard as it looks.

Thanks to a brave man named Joshua, who was strong enough to tell Sara the truth and make her face herself and accept herself for who she is. He revealed to Sara that no one is worth not being yourself to please others.

Everyone has their thing to hide, and their concerns, but still, there are always those ready to take advantage of the ones who feel they should be ashamed of who they are and the way God created them.

Thanks to Joshua for saving this woman.